Julia Donaldson
Princess Mirror-Belle

Illustrated by **Lydia Monks**

MACMILLAN CHILDREN'S BOOKS

For Phoebe

First published 2003 by Macmillan Children's Books

This edition published 2013 by Macmillan Children's Books
a division of Macmillan Publishers Limited
20 New Wharf Road, London N1 9RR
Basingstoke and Oxford
Associated companies throughout the world
www.panmacmillan.com

ISBN 978-1-4472-2402-0

Text copyright © Julia Donaldson 2003
Illustrations copyright © Lydia Monks 2003

The right of Julia Donaldson and Lydia Monks to be identified as the
author and illustrator of this work has been asserted by them in
accordance with the Copyright, Designs and Patents Act 1988.

1 3 5 7 9 8 6 4 2

A CIP catalogue record for this book is available from the British Library.

Printed and bound by CPI Group (UK) Ltd, Croydon CR0 4YY

Julia
2013,
author
children
classic *Th*
copies wor
and songs
always in den
husband and t

Lydia Monks is o
book artists worki
colour and collage
and several awards,
Her recent collabora
include *What the Lady*
Rabbit. Lydia was born in Surrey and studied Illustration at Kingston University; a keen Irish dancer, she now lives in Sheffield with her partner and their daughter.

9030 00003 0654 2

Contents

Chapter One

DRAGONPOX

"You've got some new ones on your face," said Ellen's mum. "Don't scratch them or you'll make them worse."

Ellen was off school with chickenpox. She didn't feel all that ill but she *did* feel sorry for herself, because she was missing the school outing to the dolphin display.

"Can you read me a story?" she asked Mum. But just then the front door bell rang.

"I'm sorry, I can't. That's Mrs Foster-Smith come for her piano lesson. Look, here are your library books . . . and remember, *no scratching*." She went out of the room.

Ellen picked up one of the books. It was full of stories about princesses. She flicked through the pages, looking at the pictures. The princesses were all very beautiful, with swirly looking clothes and hair down to their waists. None of them had chickenpox. Ellen started to read *The Sleeping Beauty*, but it was difficult to concentrate. For one thing, her spots were so itchy. For another, Mrs Foster-Smith was thumping away at "The Fairies' Dance" on the piano downstairs. The way she played it, it sounded more like "The Elephants' Dance".

Ellen decided to have a look at her new spots. There was no mirror in her bedroom so she put on her right slipper (she had lost her left one) and padded into the bathroom.

She studied her face in the mirror over

the basin. One of the new spots was right in the middle of her nose. The more Ellen looked at it, the itchier it felt . . . . Her hand crept towards it. Just a little *tiny* scratch wouldn't matter, surely. Her finger was just about to touch the spot when a strange thing happened. Her reflection dodged to one side and said, "Don't scratch or you'll turn into a toad!"

Ellen didn't reply. She was too surprised. She just stared.

"I've never *seen* such a bad case of dragonpox," said the mirror girl.

"It's not dragonpox, it's *chicken*pox,"

Ellen found herself saying. "Anyway, yours is just as bad – you're my reflection."

"Don't be silly, I'm not you," said the mirror girl, and to prove it she stuck one hand out of the mirror and then the other.

"Come on, help me out," she said, reaching for Ellen's hand.

Ellen gave a gentle pull and the mirror girl climbed out of the mirror, into the basin and down on to the bathroom floor.

"What a funny little room!" she said.

"It's not *that* little!" said Ellen. This was true – there was room in the bathroom for three of the tall pot plants that

Mum was so keen on.

The mirror girl laughed. "The bathroom in the palace is about ten times this size," she said.

"The *palace*?" repeated Ellen.

"Of course. Where would you expect a princess to live?"

"Are you a princess, then?"

"I most certainly am. I'm Princess Mirror-Belle. You really ought to curtsy, but as you're my friend I'll let you off."

"But . . . you don't *look* like a princess," said Ellen. "You look just like me. You've got the same pyjamas and just one slipper. You've even got a plaster on your finger like me."

"These are just my dressing-up clothes," said Mirror-Belle. "In the palace I usually wear a dress of silver silk, like the moon." She thought for a moment and then added, "Or one of golden satin, like the sun. And anyway, my slipper's on my *left* foot and my plaster's on my *right* finger. Yours are the other way round."

Ellen didn't see that this made much difference, but she didn't want to get into an argument, so instead she asked Mirror-Belle, "Why have you got the plaster? Did you cut yourself on the bread knife like me?"

"No, of course not," said Mirror-Belle. "I was pricked on my finger by a wicked fairy."

"Just like the Sleeping Beauty!" said Ellen. "Did you go to sleep for a hundred years too?"

"No – two hundred," said Mirror-Belle. "I only woke up this morning." She gave a huge yawn as if to prove it.

"Did you put the plaster on before you went to sleep or after you woke up?" asked Ellen, but Mirror-Belle didn't seem to want to answer this question. Instead she put the plug into the bath and turned on the taps.

"Hey, what are you doing?" asked Ellen.

"Getting the cure ready, what do you think?"

"What cure?"

"The cure for dragonpox, of course."

"But I haven't got dragonpox!"

"Well, I have," said Mirror-Belle, "and I'll tell you how I got it. I was in the palace garden last week, playing with my golden ball, when—"

"Weren't you still asleep last week?" Ellen interrupted. "Didn't you say you only woke up this morning?"

"I wish you'd stop asking so many questions. As I was about to say, an enormous dragon flew down and captured me. Luckily a knight came and rescued me, but when I got back to the palace I came out in all these spots. My mother the Queen sent for the doctor and he said I'd caught dragonpox."

"Well, my doctor said mine were chickenpox," said Ellen.

"I suppose you were captured by a chicken, were you?" said Mirror-Belle. "Not quite so exciting, really. Still, I expect the cure's just the same." She picked up a bottle of bubble bath and poured nearly all of it into the water.

"That's far too much!" shrieked Ellen. But Mirror-Belle was too busy investigating the cupboard on the wall to answer.

"This looks good too," she said.

"But that's my dad's shaving cream," said Ellen.

"It's nice and frothy," said Mirror-Belle, squirting some into the bath. "And *this* looks just the job," she said, taking the cap off a tube of Minty-Zing toothpaste, which had red and green stripes.

"Nice colours," said Mirror-Belle, squeezing most of the toothpaste out into the bath.

Ellen was a bit shocked at first but

then she giggled.

"Shall we put some of Luke's hair gel in too?" she asked. Ellen's big brother had started getting interested in his appearance recently and was always smoothing  bright blue sticky stuff into his hair.

"Good idea," said Mirror-Belle. Ellen scooped the gel out of the tube and into the bath. That would serve Luke right for all the times he'd hogged the hair-dryer.

Mirror-Belle poured in a bottle of orange-coloured shampoo and eyed the bath water thoughtfully. "We still need one more ingredient," she said. "*I* know!" She picked up Mum's bottle of Blue Moon perfume and began spraying merrily.

Ellen, who had begun to enjoy herself, felt rather alarmed again. Mum only ever put a tiny bit of Blue Moon behind her ears. By now the bathroom smelt like a flower shop.

"Let's get in now," said Mirror-Belle. In another moment the two of them were up to their chests in bubbles, cream, gel and toothpaste.

"I can feel the cure working already, can't you?" said Mirror-Belle, and flipped some froth at Ellen. Ellen flipped some back, and a blob of toothpaste landed on the spot on Mirror-Belle's nose.

Ellen noticed that Mirror-Belle, like herself, had a pale mark round one of her wrists.

"We've both got watch-strap marks," she said. "Did you lose your watch like I did?"

Mirror-Belle looked at her grandly and said, "This mark isn't from a *watch*. Oh no. It's from my magic wishing bangle."

"A wishing bangle! Can you wish for anything you want?"

"Naturally," said Mirror-Belle. "And for things that other people *don't* want."

"Such as?"

"Well, once I wished for a worm in the palace garden to grow to the size of a snake and give the gardener a fright."

"And did it?"

"Yes. The only trouble was, it didn't stop growing. It grew and grew till it took up the whole of the garden. Then we had to banish it to an island, but it *still* kept growing."

"But couldn't you just wish it small again?"

Mirror-Belle looked annoyed for a second but then her face cleared and she said, "No, because I dropped the bangle in the sea and it got swallowed by a fish. Luckily, though, I caught the

fish last week."

Ellen thought of reminding her once again that she had said she was asleep last week, but she decided not to. It would only make Mirror-Belle cross. It was more fun just to listen to her stories, even if some of them sounded a bit like fibs.

"I don't feel quite so bad about missing the dolphin display any more," she said.

"Is *that* all you're missing?" asked Mirror-Belle. "*I'm* missing the sea monster display."

The two of them played at being dolphins and sea monsters for a while, splashing a lot of water and froth out of the bath.

"Your dragonpox hasn't gone away yet," said Ellen.

"Don't be so impatient," said Mirror-Belle. "We haven't done Stage Two yet."

"What's that?"

"Get out and I'll show you," said

Mirror-Belle. They both got out of the bath and Mirror-Belle picked up a roll of toilet paper. She began winding it round and round Ellen, starting with her legs and working upwards.

"I feel like an Egyptian mummy," said Ellen, laughing.

Mirror-Belle reached Ellen's face. She wound the paper round and round until Ellen couldn't see out.

"Now you have to count to a hundred," she said.

"What about you?" asked Ellen.

"We'll do me later," said Mirror-Belle.

Ellen started to count. She could hear Mirror-Belle moving

about the room and from downstairs came the sound of Mrs Foster-Smith playing "The Babbling Brook". The way she played it, it sounded more like "The Crashing Ocean".

When Ellen got to about eighty she heard Mirror-Belle say something which sounded like, "Ow! Stupid old taps!"

When she got to a hundred she tried to unwind the toilet paper but it got into a tangle.

"Help me, Mirror-Belle," she said. But there was silence.

Ellen managed to tear the toilet paper away from her eyes, but Mirror-Belle was nowhere to be seen.

"Mirror-Belle! Where are you?" called Ellen. Mirror-Belle's pyjamas had disappeared as well. Could she have put them on and gone out of the room?

Ellen opened the door. Maybe Mirror-Belle had gone downstairs. Ellen was still half-wrapped in toilet paper but she didn't bother about that. She set off downstairs in search of Mirror-Belle.

When she was six stairs from the bottom, two things happened. Ellen tripped up and fell down the stairs, and Mrs Foster-Smith came out of the sitting room. Ellen went crashing into her, and Mrs Foster-Smith let out a shriek.

"Ellen! What *are* you up to?" asked Mum, following Mrs Foster-Smith out of the room.

"It's Stage Two. It's all to do with dragonpox," Ellen began explaining. "Mirror-Belle said that the cure for chickenpox was just the same. You need bubble bath and toothpaste and hair gel and . . ."

"The child's raving – she's delirious," said Mrs Foster-Smith. "I think we ought to call the doctor."

"I don't think it's that bad," said Mum. "Go and put your pyjamas back on, Ellen, and I'll be with you in a minute. I'll see you at the same time next week then, Mrs Foster-Smith. And as I said, maybe you could try playing the pieces just a *little* more quietly."

Back in the bathroom, Ellen finished untangling herself. She had just got into her pyjamas when Mum came into the room. She looked round in horror at the empty jars and bottles and the froth everywhere.

"What a horrible mess!" she said.

"It wasn't me – not much of it, any-way. It was Mirror-Belle. She came out of the mirror."

"Oh yes, and I suppose she's gone back into it now."

Ellen looked at the mirror. It was covered in toothpasty bubbles.

"I think you're right," she said.

Mum wiped the bubbles off the mirror. Ellen looked into it. The girl she saw there *did* look like Mirror-Belle, but she moved whenever Ellen moved: it was just her own reflection.

Ellen frowned, suddenly unsure about everything. She couldn't just have imagined Mirror-Belle, could she? Her reflection frowned back.

Mum scurried round the room, tut-tutting and clearing up the mess. The worst part was when she discovered how little of her Blue Moon perfume was left.

"I know I leave you on your own a lot when I do my piano-teaching, but I *did* think you were old enough not to do things like this," she said. "You should be in bed with those chickenpox – though I must say, they do look quite a bit better. That big one on your nose seems to have disappeared!"

Then she caught sight of something in the basin and, looking surprised, picked it up.

"Look – here's your left slipper!" she said. "I'm glad it's turned up at last."

Ellen didn't say anything (that would

only annoy Mum again) but she smiled
to herself as she put the slipper on,
because she knew whose slipper it really
was.

Chapter Two

ELLEN'S CASTLE

Ellen and her mother were in one of the changing rooms of a big department store. They were supposed to be buying a dress for Ellen to wear to her grown-up cousin's wedding, but nothing seemed to fit or look right.

"That greeny-blue colour suits you," said Ellen's mum, "but it's too tight. I'll go and see if they've got a bigger size."

Ellen didn't really care *what* dress she wore to the wedding. No one would be looking at her, since she hadn't been asked to be a bridesmaid – something she felt a bit cross about. She practised

making her most hideous face at herself
in the mirror – the one where her eyeballs rolled up and almost out of sight and
her bottom lip jutted over the top one. If
she did that at the wedding, people *would*
look at her. But of course she'd be too shy
to do it when the time came.

This time, though, the face didn't seem

to be working properly. The eyeballs in
the mirror rolled back to normal, the
mouth went back to its ordinary shape,
then opened and said, "You look just like
that wicked fairy – the one who pricked
my finger."

"Mirror-Belle!" exclaimed Ellen. "What are you doing here?"

Mirror-Belle stepped out of the mirror. She was wearing a too-tight, greeny-blue dress just like the one Ellen had on.

"I see you've moved house," she said, looking around her.

"This isn't a house, it's a shop," said Ellen, but Mirror-Belle wasn't listening. She had picked up Ellen's coat from the floor where it was lying inside out, and was putting it on that way, so that the tartan lining was on the out-side.

"Not bad," she said, looking at her reflection. Then, "Come on, let's see what your cook has made for lunch." And she walked out

of the changing room.
"No! Stop!" cried
Ellen. "Give me back
my coat!" She ran
after Mirror-Belle,
who was merrily
weaving her way
around the rails and stands of clothes.

"You *have* got a lot of clothes," she
said when Ellen caught up with her.
"Almost as many as me, though not
such beautiful ones, of course. I don't
suppose you've got a ballgown made of
rose petals stitched together with spider's thread, have you?"

"No, I haven't," said Ellen. "But I don't
think I'd want one. Wouldn't the rose
petals shrivel up and die?"

Mirror-Belle thought for a moment
and then said, "No, they've been dipped
in a magic fountain which keeps them
fresh for ever."

By this stage they had reached the escalator. Mirror-Belle hopped on to it.

"This is fun," she said. "Does it go down to the dungeons?"

"No," said Ellen, riding down beside her. "It goes down to the food department."

"The banqueting hall, do you mean?" asked Mirror-Belle. "Oh good, I'm starving."

She skipped off the escalator. They were in the fruit and vegetable section of the food department. Mirror-Belle picked up a potato and put it down again in disgust.

"It's *raw*!" she said. "How does your cook expect us to eat that?" She inspected the cabbages and cauliflowers. "What sort of banquet is *this* supposed to be?" she asked. "None of the food is cooked at all."

"It's not *supposed* to be cooked – people take it home to cook," Ellen tried to explain. "Look, Mirror-Belle, do give me back my raincoat – I must get back to Mum."

"These apples look all right," said Mirror-Belle, picking one up and taking a large bite out of it. She picked up another one and did the same. "With green and red apples like these I only ever bite the green side," she explained. "You can't be too careful – there could be a wicked queen going round putting poison into the red sides. Look what happened to my friend Snow White." She took a bite out of another apple.

Just then a shop assistant came up.

"Stop eating the fruit," she said to Mirror-Belle.

"Start cooking the vegetables!" Mirror-Belle said back to her.

The shop assistant looked startled, and asked Mirror-Belle where her mum or dad was.

"Sitting on their thrones, I expect," said Mirror-Belle. "Come on, Ellen, let's go and play in your bedroom." She grabbed Ellen's hand and pulled her into a lift.

"Does this go up to the battlements?" she asked as the doors closed.

"No," said Ellen. "You seem to think this is some kind of castle but it's not, it's a—"

"Ah, *here's* your bedroom," said Mirror-Belle as the lift doors opened on the second floor. They were in the furniture department. Mirror-Belle darted past some armchairs and sofas to an area full of beds and mattresses. She flung herself

down on a double bed and almost immediately sprang off it again.

"I hope you don't sleep on *that* one,"
she said. "I certainly couldn't
sleep a wink on it."

"No, I don't," said Ellen.
"This isn't my—"

"Good," said Mirror-Belle,
"because there's a pea under the mattress."

"How do you know?"

"We princesses can always tell," said
Mirror-Belle, and she flopped down on to
another bed. "Ugh!" she said. "There's a
baked bean under this one – horribly
lumpy. Lie down and maybe you'll be
able to feel it too."

Ellen giggled. She looked around.
There wasn't a shop assistant in sight.
She lay down on the bed next to Mirror-
Belle. It felt wonderfully springy and
comfortable.

"I can't feel anything," she said.

"That must be because you're not a princess," said Mirror-Belle. "Ordinary people have to bounce to detect peas and beans under mattresses. Like this." She got to her feet and began to jump up and down on the bed.

"Come on!" she said.

Ellen looked around again. There were still no shop assistants to be seen. She joined Mirror-Belle and soon the two of them were bouncing about on the bed,

making the springs of the mattress twang.

"This is nearly as good as the school trampoline," said Ellen breathlessly.

"It's not as good as the *palace* trampoline," said Mirror-Belle. "I once bounced right up into the clouds from that."

"Did you come down all right?"

"No, I didn't," said Mirror-Belle. "The North Wind saw me up there and swept me away to the land of ice."

"What happened then?"

But Ellen never found out because at that moment an angry-looking shop assistant came towards them.

"Quick! Let's run!" Ellen said. But Mirror-Belle had a different idea. She jumped off the bed and advanced towards the assistant as angrily as he was advancing towards them.

"Ah, there you are at last!" she said, before he had a chance to speak. "I want to complain about the state of this bedroom. Peas and beans under all the mattresses – it's disgraceful! Set to work removing them immediately or you'll be fired from the castle!" And with that she linked her arm in Ellen's, turned and strode off towards the escalator. The shop assistant was left gawping as they sailed up to the toy department.

"So this is your playroom, is it?" asked Mirror-Belle.

Ellen tried to explain that they weren't *her* toys, but Mirror-Belle was already emptying the pieces of a jigsaw puzzle out on to the floor.

"Too much sky in this one," she said, and moved on.

"Aren't you going to clear it up?" asked Ellen.

"What, and let your lazy servants get even lazier? Certainly not."

Mirror-Belle continued down the aisle of toys, emptying out various boxes, not

satisfied till she
reach... a shelf full
of cuddly toys.
There were teddies
and rabbits, pup-
pies and monkeys,
but Mirror-Belle
picked up a furry
green frog and
kissed it on the nose.

"Why are you doing that?" asked Ellen.

"I'm turning him into a prince," said
Mirror-Belle. "Princesses can do that,
you know."

"Even *furry* frogs?"

"Yes, they just turn into furry princes,
that's all. This one seems to want to stay
a frog, though," said Mirror-Belle. "All
right, you silly creature, away you leap,"
and she threw the frog across the shop
and turned her attention to a teddy.

"I've never tried it on a bear," she said.

But Ellen had noticed a man coming towards them from about where the frog must have landed. He looked even crosser than the bed man had done. She tugged at Mirror-Belle's sleeve in alarm, but Mirror-Belle looked delighted to see the man.

"Don't you see, it's the *prince*," she said. "He doesn't look a very nice prince, mind you," she went on as the man drew closer. "You're not very furry either," as he came right up to them, "unless you count your funny woolly moustache."

"What do you think you're doing?" the man asked.

"Aren't you going to say thank you?" Mirror-Belle said to him.

"What, for throwing toys around?"

"No, for breaking the spell, of course," said Mirror-Belle. "Though if I'd known what a bad-tempered prince you'd turn out to be I wouldn't have bothered. Can't say I blame that witch for turning you into a frog in the first place. Come on, Ellen!"

She turned and walked briskly away, calling over her shoulder, "And if you think you're going to marry me you've got another think coming."

The man stood rooted to the spot for a few moments, too astounded to follow them. By the time he did, Mirror-Belle and Ellen had dived into a lift. Mirror-Belle pressed the top button.

"Perhaps *this*'ll take us to the battlements at last," she said.

"It says 'Offices Only'," said Ellen.

When they got out they were in a corridor with a few doors leading off it. One of the doors was ajar and Ellen could hear a familiar voice coming from it.

"I only went out for a couple of minutes to look for another dress, and when

I got back she'd gone." Ellen couldn't bear to hear Mum sounding so upset.

"Come with me," she said to Mirror-Belle and ran into the room. Her mother was there with another lady.

"Oh *there* you are, darling," said Mum, hugging her. "Where *have* you been?"

"With Mirror-Belle. She took my coat so I had to follow her," said Ellen. "She's just outside." She took her mother's hand and pulled her into the corridor. There was no one there.

"You didn't mention another little girl," said the shop lady to Mum.

"There isn't one really – it's just my daughter's imaginary friend."

"She's not imaginary, she's real," Ellen protested.

The light outside the lift showed that it was still on the top floor. "She must be in here," said Ellen, pressing the button.

The doors opened. Apart from a crumpled raincoat with a tartan lining lying on the floor, the lift was empty. Where on earth was Princess Mirror-Belle?

It was only then that Ellen noticed something which she should have spotted before.

The walls of the lift were covered in mirrors.

Princess Mirror-Belle had disappeared!

Chapter Three

SNOW WHITE AND THE EIGHT DWARFS

Ellen's big brother Luke was singing again.

"Seven little hats on seven little heads. Seven little pillows on seven little beds," he sang, standing on a ladder and dabbing paint on to the branches of a canvas tree. A blob of paint landed on Ellen's hand. She was squatting on the stage, painting the tree trunk.

Ellen sighed heavily – more because of the song than the blob of paint. Luke had been singing the seven dwarfs' song almost non-stop ever since he'd joined the local drama group and got a part in the Christmas pantomime.

"Seven pairs of trousers on fourteen little legs," he sang now.

"No one could call *your* legs little," said Ellen. "You should be acting a giant, not a dwarf."

"There aren't any giants in *Snow White*, dumbo," said Luke. "Anyway, I told you, we all walk about on our knees."

"So that Sally Hart can pat you on the head," said Ellen. She knew that Luke was keen on Sally Hart. In fact, she guessed that he was only in the pantomime because Sally was acting Snow White.

Luke blushed but all he said was, "Shut up or I won't get you a ticket for tonight."

The first performance of *Snow White* was that evening, and at the last minute the director had decided that the forest needed a couple of extra trees. Luke had volunteered to go and paint them, and Mum had persuaded him to take Ellen along.

Although Ellen was too shy to want to be in the play, it was fun being in the theatre in front of all the rows of empty seats. But Luke wouldn't let her have a go on the ladder, and soon she had painted the bottom of the two tree trunks.

Luke was getting quite carried away with the leaves and acorns, still singing the annoying song all the time. He didn't seem to notice when Ellen wandered off to explore the theatre. She opened a door in a narrow passageway behind the stage.

The room was dark and Ellen switched on the light – or rather, the lights: there was a whole row of bulbs, all shining brightly above a long mirror. This must be one of the dressing rooms.

Some beards were hanging up on a row

of hooks. Ellen guessed they belonged to the seven dwarfs. She unhooked one and tried it on. It was quite tickly.

"Seven little beards on seven little chins," she sang into the mirror.

"And seven mouldy cauliflowers in seven smelly bins," her reflection sang back at her.

But of course it wasn't her reflection. It was Princess Mirror-Belle.

Quickly, Ellen turned her back, hoping that Mirror-Belle would stay in the mirror. Mirror-Belle was the last person she wanted to see just now. Their adventures together always seemed to land Ellen in trouble.

But it was too late. Mirror-Belle had climbed out of the mirror and was tapping Ellen on the shoulder.

"Let's have a look at your beard," she said, and then, as Ellen turned round, "I'd shave it off if I were you – it doesn't suit you."

"It's only a play one," said Ellen. "Anyway, you've got one too."

"I know." Mirror-Belle sighed. "The hairdresser said the wrong spell and I ended up with a beard instead of short hair."

"Couldn't the hairdresser use scissors instead of spells?" asked Ellen.

"Good heavens no," said Mirror-Belle. "An ordinary one could, maybe, but this is the *palace* hairdresser we're talking about."

She turned to a rail of costumes, pulled a robin outfit off its hanger and held it up against herself.

"Put that back!" cried Ellen, and then, "You'll get it all painty!"

They both looked at Mirror-Belle's left hand, which had paint on it, just like Ellen's right one.

"Have you been painting trees too?" Ellen asked.

"No, of course not." Mirror-Belle looked thoughtful as she hung the robin costume back on the rail. Then, "No – trees have been painting *me*," she said.

Ellen couldn't help laughing. "How can they do *that*?" she asked.

"Not *all* trees can do it," replied Mirror-Belle. "Just

the ones in the magic forest. They bend down their branches and dip them into the muddy lake and paint anyone who comes past."

"How strange," said Ellen.

"I don't think it's so strange as people painting trees, which is what you say you've been doing," said Mirror-Belle.

"They're not real trees," Ellen explained. "They're for a play."

Mirror-Belle looked quite interested. "Can I help?" she asked.

"No, you certainly can't," said Ellen, horrified, but Mirror-Belle wasn't put off.

"What sort of trees are they?" she asked. "I'm very good at painting bananas. And pineapples."

"Pineapples don't grow on trees, and anyway—" but Ellen broke off because she heard the stage door bang.

"Ellen! Where are you?" came Luke's voice.

"I'm coming!" Ellen yelled. Then she hissed to Mirror-Belle, "Get back into the mirror! Don't mess about with the costumes! And *stay away from the trees*!"

That evening Ellen was back in the theatre, sitting in the audience next to Mum and Dad. *Snow White* was about to start.

Mum squeezed Ellen's hand. "You look nervous," she said. "Don't worry – I'm sure Luke will be fine."

But it wasn't Luke that Ellen was nervous about – it was Mirror-Belle. What had she been up to in the empty theatre all afternoon? Ellen was terrified that when the curtain went up, the trees would be covered in tropical fruit and the costumes would be covered in paint.

The curtain went up. There were no bananas or pineapples to be seen. The forest looked beautiful. Dad leaned across Mum's seat and whispered, "Very well-painted trees, Ellen."

Sally Hart – or rather, Snow White – looked beautiful too, with her black hair, big eyes and rosy cheeks. Over her arm she carried a basket, and she fed bread-crumbs to a chorus of hungry robins. None of them seemed to have paint on their costumes.

Ellen breathed a sigh of relief.

Everything was all right after all! Mirror-Belle must have gone back into the dressing-room mirror.

A palace scene came next. When the wicked Queen looked into her magic mirror and asked,

"Mirror, mirror on the wall,

Who is the fairest one of all?"

for an awful moment Ellen was afraid that Mirror-Belle might come leaping out of the mirror, shouting "I am!" But of course she could only do that if it was *Ellen* looking into the mirror. Stop being so jumpy, Ellen told herself – Mirror-Belle is safely back in her own world.

When the scene changed to the dwarfs' cottage, Mum gave Ellen a nudge. Soon Luke would be coming on stage!

And yes, now Snow White was asleep in one of the beds, and here came the dwarfs, shuffling in through the cottage door. Ellen knew that they were walking on their knees but the costumes were so good, with shoes stitched on to the front of the baggy trousers, that you couldn't really tell.

Luke was acting the bossiest dwarf – typical, Ellen thought. He told the others to hang up their jackets and set the table. Then they started to dance around and sing the song that Ellen was so tired of hearing.

"Seven little jackets on seven little pegs. Seven little eggcups, and seven little eggs."

But something was wrong. One of the dwarfs was singing much louder than the others, and not getting all the words right. When the other dwarfs stopped singing and started to tap out the tune on the table, the dwarf with the loud voice carried on:

"Seven stupid people who don't know how to count. Can't they see that seven

is not the right amount?"

The audience laughed as they realised that there were *eight* dwarfs and not seven. But Ellen didn't laugh. Dwarf number eight had to be Mirror-Belle, and there was bound to be serious trouble ahead.

Up on the stage, Luke looked furious. He stopped tapping the table and started chasing Mirror-Belle round the room. He was trying to chase her out of the door but she kept dodging him as she carried on singing:

"Eight little spoons and eight little bowls. Sixteen little woolly socks with sixteen great big holes."

Ellen felt like shouting, or throwing

something, or rushing on to the stage herself and dragging Mirror-Belle off. But that would just make things worse. All she could do was to watch in horror.

In the end, Luke gave up the chase. With one last glare at Mirror-Belle he strode over to the bed where Snow White was sleeping. His cross expression changed to one of adoration when Snow White woke up and sang a song.

"Will you stay with us?" Luke begged her when the song had finished.

"Yes, do stay and look after us," said another dwarf.

"We need someone to comb our beards."

"And wash our clothes."

"And shine our shoes."

"And cook our meals."

"And clean our house."

All the dwarfs except Mirror-Belle were chiming in.

"There's nothing I'd like better!" exclaimed Snow White.

Mirror-Belle turned on her. "You must be joking," she said angrily. "You shouldn't be doing things like that – you're a *princess*! You should be bossing *them* about, not the other way round."

The audience laughed – except for Ellen – and Snow White's mouth fell open. Ellen felt sorry for her: she obviously didn't know what to say. But Luke came to the rescue.

"Be quiet!" he ordered Mirror-Belle.

"You don't know anything about princesses."

"Of course I do — I *am* one!" Mirror-Belle retorted. "I'm just in disguise as a dwarf. I thought Snow White might need some protection against that horrible Queen. I'm pretty sure she's going to be along soon with a tray of poisoned apples, and—"

"Shut up, you're spoiling the story!" hissed Luke, and put a hand over Mirror-Belle's mouth. Snow White looked at him in admiration. Luke made a sign to someone offstage, and a second later the curtain came down. It was the end of the first half.

"Isn't Luke good?" said Mum in the interval. "He never told us he had such a big part."

"That little girl playing the extra dwarf is a hoot, isn't she?" said Dad.

"She sounds a bit like you, Ellen. Who is she?"

"I don't know," muttered Ellen. It was no use mentioning Mirror-Belle to her parents, who just thought she was an imaginary friend. Ellen licked her ice cream but she was too worried to enjoy it properly. What would Mirror-Belle get up to in the second half of the show?

The curtain went up again. Snow White was sweeping the dwarfs' cottage. Ellen was relieved that there was no sign of Mirror-Belle. She must have gone off to work with the other dwarfs.

The wicked Queen appeared at the cottage window. She looked quite different – like an old woman – as she held out a tray of apples and offered one to Snow White.

"The dwarfs made me promise not to buy anything from a stranger," said Snow White.

"There's no need to buy," replied the disguised Queen. "Just open the window, and I'll give you one!"

Snow White opened the window and took an apple in her hand. She still looked doubtful.

"Don't you trust me?" asked the Queen. "Look, I'll take a bite out of it myself first to prove that it's all right." She did this and handed the apple back to Snow White.

Snow White had just opened her mouth when a voice cried, "Stop!" and a second figure appeared at the cottage window. Oh no! It was Mirror-Belle.

"Stop! Don't you realise, she took that bite out of the green half of the apple. It's the red half that's poisoned!" she warned Snow White.

Snow White took no notice and was about to bite into the apple when

Mirror-Belle snatched it from her. She snatched the tray of apples from the Queen too. The next moment she had burst in through the cottage door, pursued by the Queen.

Some steps led down from the stage into the audience, and Mirror-Belle ran down them. She ran through the audience, the Queen hot on her heels.

When Mirror-Belle reached Ellen's

seat she whispered, "Here, take this!" and thrust the tray of apples on to Ellen's lap. Ellen didn't know what to do, but was saved from doing anything by the Queen, who snatched the tray back. Mirror-Belle grabbed it from her again and ran on.

Meanwhile, Snow White, who had run off the back of the stage, reappeared holding Luke's hand and followed by the other dwarfs. They joined in the chase, round and round the audience and back on to the stage. Luke overtook the others. He caught Mirror-Belle by the shoulders and shook her.

"Give back those apples!" he ordered.

"What! Do you *want* Snow White to be poisoned?" protested Mirror-Belle. "Some friend you are!"

"Who is she, anyway?" asked Snow White – except that she didn't sound like Snow White any more, she sounded like

Sally Hart.

"I don't know but we'll soon find out!" said Luke – sounding like Luke and not a dwarf – and he ripped Mirror-Belle's beard off.

"Ellen, it's you!" he exclaimed.

"Oh no I'm not!" said Mirror-Belle. "Your sister Ellen is in the audience – there, look!" She pointed, and to Ellen's embarrassment not only Luke but everyone else on the stage and in the audience was looking at her.

Not for long, though. Soon all eyes were back on Mirror-Belle, who was throwing apples into the audience.

"Don't eat them, *and don't give them back*!" she ordered.

Just then a man in a suit came on to the stage. Ellen recognised him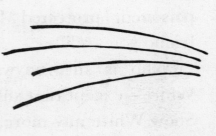

as Mr Turnbull, the director. He strode up to Mirror-Belle.

"I don't know who you are or where you come from, but you'd better go back there before I call the police!" he said.

"Don't worry, I will!" said Mirror-Belle. Mr Turnbull made a grab for her but she dodged him and ran out through the cottage door. Mr Turnbull and all the actors followed her, and Ellen heard the Queen shout, "Oh no! She's got my mirror now!"

A moment later, Mirror-Belle was climbing back into the cottage through the open window, clutching the Queen's mirror. She scuttled into the dwarfs' cupboard just as everyone else came charging back in through the door.

 "Where is she?" asked Mr Turnbull, with his back to the cupboard. Mirror-Belle popped her head out.

"She's behind you!" yelled the audience. Mr Turnbull turned round but now the cupboard door was shut.

"Oh no she's not!" said Mr Turnbull.

"OH YES SHE IS!" the audience shouted back.

Snow White opened the cupboard door and peered in.

"Is she there?" asked Mr Turnbull.

"I don't think so," said Snow White. She picked up her broom and swept around inside, just to make sure. "What's this?" she asked, as she swept an object out of the cupboard.

"It's my magic mirror!" said the Queen. "So she must have been here."

"Well, she's gone now, thank goodness," said Mr Turnbull. He turned to face the audience.

"I'm sorry about all this, ladies and gentlemen," he said. "Anyone who wants their money back can ask at the box

office. But now, on with the show!"

"Seven little cups and seven little plates," sang Mum next day, as she served up Ellen's lunch. Luke was having a lie-in.

"Oh, Mum, don't *you* start!"

"Sorry. Wasn't Luke brilliant last night? I can't wait to show him the piece in the paper."

"Let's have a look."

Mum passed Ellen the paper, and this is what she read:

"The Pinkerton Players' performance of *Snow White* last night was a comic triumph. The hilarious chase scene was hugely enjoyable, and so was the entertaining scene in which the director pretended to offer the audience their money back.

"All the cast gave excellent performances, especially Sally Hart as Snow White and Luke Page as the bossy dwarf, but the real star of the show was the child who played the Eighth Dwarf. Sadly, she was not present at the curtain call. Perhaps she was too young to stay up so late.

"I have only one criticism of the show. Why did this child star's name not appear in the programme? Everyone wants to know who she is, and everyone wants to see more of her."

Yes, thought Ellen. Everyone except me.

Chapter Four

PARTY HOPPERS

"Happy birthday, Anthony," said Ellen, holding out a present. Her six-year-old cousin snatched it and ripped off the paper.

"It's a book! I hate books – they're boring," he said, throwing it on the floor. "Why couldn't you get me a video?"

Anthony was a pain, and the most painful thing about him was that he was exactly two years younger than Ellen's friend Livvy. Their parties were on the same day, and Mum always insisted that Ellen went to Anthony's one. It just wasn't fair – especially this year, when

Livvy's eighth birthday party was in the swimming pool, with inflatables to bounce about on and pizzas in the café afterwards.

"Let's play a few games before tea," said Anthony's mother, Auntie Pam, brightly. Ellen's heart sank even lower. The games were always the same – Stick the Tail on the Donkey, Pass the Parcel and Musical Chairs, and Anthony always won at least two of them – his mother saw to that.

Auntie Pam stuck up a big picture of a donkey without a tail and gave each child a paper tail with their name written on it.

"How about you going first, as you're the oldest, Ellen?" she suggested. She tied a scarf round Ellen's eyes and guided her towards the donkey picture. Ellen pinned the tail on to it blindly and everyone laughed. Auntie Pam removed the scarf and Ellen saw that the tail was sticking on to one of the donkey's ears.

All the other guests had goes, till the donkey had tails growing out of its legs, mane and nose. Then it was Anthony's turn. "Don't tie it too tight!" he ordered his mother. When he was standing in front of the donkey picture Ellen noticed him tilting his head back and she guessed that he was peeping out from below the scarf. Sure enough, he stuck the tail on to exactly the right spot.

"Brilliant, birthday boy!" said Auntie Pam, and presented him with the prize, which was an enormous box of chocolates.

"Now let's play Dead Lions," she said. This was a game where you all had to lie on the floor and try not to move. If you moved you were Out – unless you were Anthony, in which case you squealed, "I didn't move, I didn't move, I *didn't*!" until your mother gave you another chance.

Auntie Pam produced a box of face paints and suggested that for a change the children might like to be different jungle animals – not just lions. She got Ellen to help her paint zebra and tiger stripes on to the younger children's faces, in front of the big mirror in the hall.

The made-up children raced back into the sitting room and Ellen was left to paint her own face. She felt in rather a poisonous mood so she decided to be a snake. She picked up the green stick and was about to start painting her face when she saw the mirror lips move and heard a familiar voice.

"Are you sure you've been invited?" asked Mirror-Belle.

Ellen felt ridiculously glad to see her. It was true that Mirror-Belle usually spelled trouble, but she was much more fun than Anthony and his friends.

"Of course I've been invited. It's my cousin's party," Ellen replied, glancing around to check that no one else could

see Mirror-Belle climbing out of the mirror.

Mirror-Belle looked around too. "Oh dear," she said. "I seem to be in the wrong place. I'm supposed to be at the wood nymphs' party. That was why I was painting my face green." Like Ellen, she had a box of face paints in one hand and a green stick in the other.

"I see you're planning to go green too," she said. "Is your cousin a wood elf or something?"

"No, he's a monster," said Ellen, and she told Mirror-Belle about Anthony and about how she really wanted to go to Livvy's swimming party.

"And so you shall!" said Mirror-Belle, sounding like the Fairy Godmother in *Cinderella*. "Off you go! I'll stay here and pretend to be you."

Ellen felt torn. "But Mirror-Belle . . . I don't know . . . could you really do that?"

"Of course," replied Mirror-Belle. "I'm an expert at pretending. In fact, I've got several gold medals for it."

Ellen could well believe that; she often wondered how many of Mirror-Belle's stories about herself were true. All the same, she was still worried about leaving her at Anthony's party.

"But you'd have to *behave* like me, not like you," she said. "You'd have to be shy and sensible, and you'd have to promise not to—" but she never finished the sentence because she heard Auntie Pam calling her.

"Coming!" said Mirror-Belle, and strode into the sitting room. There was no choice left. Ellen crept to the front door and let herself out.

The swimming pool wasn't far from Anthony's house. Ellen ran all the way. Livvy and the other guests had only just arrived, and Livvy's mother was giving them all 20p pieces for the lockers.

"Ellen!" shouted Livvy. "That's brilliant – I thought you had to go to your cousin's party. Where are your swimming things?"

"Oh dear. I left them at home," said Ellen. She felt foolish, particularly as she was still clutching the box of face paints.

"Shall I phone your mother and ask her to bring them round?" offered Livvy's mother.

"Er . . . no, she's gone out," said Ellen.

"Well, never mind – I expect you can borrow a costume and towel from Lost Property," and Livvy's mother went off to organise this.

"Is that my present? I love face paints!" said Livvy.

"Er, yes," said Ellen, thrusting the box into her hands. "I'm sorry I didn't have time to wrap them up." She'd never told Livvy about Mirror-Belle and this didn't seem a good time to start.

The Lost Property costume was a bit loose but Ellen didn't

mind. It was wonderful to be in the water with Livvy and the others. They had the pool all to themselves. There was a huge inflatable sea monster, and a pirate ship and a desert island. Livvy made up a really good game called Sharks, where you had to swim from the desert island to the ship without being caught by a shark. If you got caught you were taken to the sea monster and had to wait on its back to be rescued. Ellen was a fast swimmer and managed to rescue several fishes from the sharks. That was fun, but the best thing about the game was that Anthony wasn't there to cheat and squeal and clamour for a prize. (There weren't any prizes, which was another good thing.)

Ellen was in the middle of a particularly daring rescue when Livvy, who was one of the sharks, grabbed her by the shoulder strap of her costume. Ellen

tried to swim away and the strap snapped.

The swimming-pool attendant beckoned to Ellen. "Pop into the changing area and they'll find you a safety pin," she said.

As Ellen fixed the strap in front of the mirror in the changing area she remembered Mirror-Belle and wondered how she was getting on at Anthony's party.

She didn't have to wonder for very long.

"Be careful with that pin," said Mirror-Belle. "You don't want to prick your finger and end up asleep for a hundred years."

At that moment Ellen felt she would like nothing better. How *could* Mirror-Belle do this to her?

"Mirror-Belle, stay there! Don't come out of the mirror! You're not supposed to be here! Go back to Anthony's party!"

"No thank you very much." Mirror-Belle jumped down beside Ellen. She too held a safety pin and wore a baggy swimming costume with a broken shoulder strap. "I couldn't stand another game of Musical Thrones," she said.

"Don't you mean Musical Chairs?" asked Ellen.

"Yes, I think that *is* what they called it," said Mirror-Belle. "Musical Thrones is much better. You leap from throne to throne, and the thrones play tunes when you land on them."

"I hope you didn't leap about on the chairs?" said Ellen.

"I did try, but it was a bit hard because Tantrummy's mother kept taking them away."

"Anthony, not Tantrummy," Ellen corrected her, though Tantrummy did seem a better name for him. "Anyway, of course his mum took the chairs away – that's the whole point of Musical Chairs: you take a chair away every time the music stops."

"Well, all that furniture-shifting seemed a lot of hard work for Tantrummy's mother," said Mirror-Belle. "She obviously needed some servants to help her. I can't think why she got so angry when I telephoned that removal firm."

Ellen gasped. "They didn't come, did they?"

"No – Tantrummy's mother cancelled

them and made us play Keep the Parcel instead."

"Pass the Parcel, you mean."

"I can't remember exactly what they called it," said Mirror-Belle, "but it took me absolutely ages to unwrap the parcel – it was a terrible waste of so much wrapping paper – and in the end there was only a tiny bag of sweets in the middle."

"But you're not supposed to unwrap the whole thing – you're just supposed to take off one wrapper and then pass it on."

"Don't be ridiculous, Ellen," said Mirror-Belle. "Didn't you know it's very rude to give away something which has been given to you?"

"I don't suppose Anthony was very

pleased when you unwrapped
the whole thing yourself."

"No, he started up a game
of his own called Scream
the House Down," said
Mirror-Belle.

Ellen almost laughed,
but then she remem-
bered that she was
the one who would
be accused of all the
things Mirror-Belle
had done.

"I hope Auntie Pam
didn't kick you out," she
said.

"No – she summoned
her magician," said
Mirror-Belle.

"Oh, was there a
conjuror? Was he
good?"

"Unfortunately not. He just did a lot of tricks – not real magic at all. In the end I had to lend him a hand."

"How do you mean?"

"He offered to make one of us disappear," said Mirror-Belle. "He had a big long box and he asked Anthony to climb into it. Then he spun the box round a few times and opened a flap. We all looked into the box and it *did* look as though Anthony had disappeared. But then I lifted a different flap and there he was!"

"That was a bit mean to spoil the trick," said Ellen.

"Wait – I haven't finished," said Mirror-Belle. "I spotted that there was a mirror inside the empty part of the box – it made that space look bigger, which was why it looked as though Anthony had disappeared."

"I'm not sure if I understand," said Ellen.

"Never mind – I'm sure you'll understand the next bit," Mirror-Belle told her. "I climbed into the part of the box with the mirror in it and told the magician to close the lid, and then . . ."

"You disappeared through the mirror!" finished Ellen.

"Precisely. The magician must be delighted. At last it looks as if he's done some real magic!"

"I shouldn't think he's delighted at *all*! He's probably horrified," said Ellen, feeling horrified herself. "They must all be looking for me! I'll have to go back there – or else you will." Oh dear, which would be worse? To send Mirror-Belle back to Anthony's or to leave her in the swimming pool?

Just then Ellen heard voices. Livvy and the others were coming to get changed. Ellen ran and opened her locker, scooped out her clothes and dived into a changing cubicle. As she closed the door she heard Livvy greet Mirror-Belle:

"What took you so long, Ellen? It's time for the pizzas now. I'm going to have ham and pineapple."

"I'll have dragon and tomato," said Mirror-Belle, and Livvy laughed.

Ellen changed quickly, and rubbed her hair as dry as she could. When she reckoned that all the others were in the cubicles she made her getaway. As she left the changing area she heard Livvy asking, "What's happened to your clothes, Ellen?" and Mirror-Belle replying, "I must have left them in the palace."

Instead of ringing Anthony's bell, Ellen crept round to the back door. It was unlocked and she tiptoed inside. She could hear voices calling her name upstairs; they must be searching the bedrooms. She peeped round the door of the sitting room. To her amazement the room was empty. On the floor was the long box which Mirror-Belle must have been talking about. Ellen lifted the lid and squeezed in. It was dark and cramped inside.

Almost immediately she heard the doorbell, followed by footsteps and voices in the hall.

"What do you mean, 'Just disappeared'?" This was her mother's voice.

"It's magic!" This was one of the children. "He's a really good conjuror. I want him to come to my party."

Then the conjuror: "It was nothing to do with me! I didn't even ask the wretched child to get into the box!"

"I want to see this box!" Mum's voice sounded really near now and Ellen realised that everyone had come into the sitting room.

"She's not there. We've looked hundreds of times," said Auntie Pam.

The next second the lid was opened and light streamed in.

"Ellen!" said Mum. Ellen climbed out and hugged her. Everyone clustered round.

"Fancy keeping her stuck in there all

that time!" Mum accused the conjuror. "And why is her hair all damp?"

"I can't understand it!" he said. "This has never happened before."

Ellen felt sorry for him. She decided to tell the truth. "It's not his fault," she said. "It was Mirror-Belle."

"Who's Mirror-Belle?" asked one of the children.

"It's Ellen's imaginary friend," explained Mum.

"What an imagination she's got!" said Auntie Pam. "She was making up all sorts of extraordinary stories earlier on." But Mum didn't hear this, because Anthony had started to clamour, "Why didn't *I* disappear? *I* want to be invisible! It's not fair – I want another go!"

When Ellen and Mum got home, Luke was on the phone.

"It's all right, here she is," Ellen heard

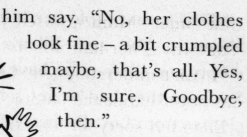

him say. "No, her clothes look fine – a bit crumpled maybe, that's all. Yes, I'm sure. Goodbye, then."

"Who was that?" asked Mum.

"This weird woman," said Luke. "Mrs Duck or someone."

"Was it Livvy Drake's mother?"

"Yes, Drake, that was it. She wanted to know if Ellen was all right."

"Why shouldn't she be all right?" asked Mum.

"Don't ask me. I couldn't understand what the woman was on about. Something about Ellen's clothes getting stolen from the swimming pool."

"But Ellen wasn't at the swimming pool."

"That's what I told her, but she kept on about it. She said Ellen's locker was empty and there must have been a thief. She said they had to get some different clothes from Lost Property."

"She's obviously mixing Ellen up with some other child," said Mum.

"And then she said Ellen just disappeared when the rest of them were eating pizzas," went on Luke. "She was worried she might have been kidnapped."

"How strange," said Mum. She gave Ellen another hug. "I think you've had quite enough adventures for one day without being kidnapped, don't you?" she asked.

"Yes," said Ellen. "I certainly do."

Chapter Five

WOBBLESDAY

Ellen hadn't seen Mirror-Belle for a few weeks. At the beginning of the summer holidays her family had moved house. The new house was in a different town, and Ellen had the feeling that Mirror-Belle had lost track of her. If so, she wasn't exactly sorry. Their adventures always seemed to end up with Ellen getting into trouble and Mirror-Belle escaping. Still, just sometimes Ellen found herself looking in the mirror and half-hoping that her reflection would do something surprising. She would have liked someone to play with. There weren't any children in either of the houses next door. A girl of about her own age lived further down the street, but Ellen was too shy to say hello. She hoped she would make some friends when she started at her new school, but she felt quite nervous about that too.

When a fair came to the common near their new house, Mum said Ellen's big brother Luke could take her as long as he stayed with her. This sounded like fun, but the trouble was that Ellen and Luke wanted to do different things. Luke liked the kind of rides where you went flying and plunging about, preferably upside down and back to front. Ellen liked being scared too, but not in an upside-down sort of way. She wanted to go on the ghost train, but Luke said that was just for kids.

"I'll see you back here in an hour, OK?" said Luke. They were in the Wobbly

Mirror Hall.

Ellen pretended to forget that Luke was supposed to stay with her.

"All right," she said. She wasn't looking at Luke but at herself in one of the wobbly mirrors. Her mouth was gaping like a cave in her droopy chin, above a long wiggly body and little waddly legs. "Look at me!" she said, laughing and pointing, but Luke had already gone. Instead, it was the peculiar reflection who replied.

"Don't point, it's rude," she said, and stepped out of the mirror.

"Mirror-Belle, it's you!" said Ellen, and laughed again. "You've gone all funny and wobbly."

"Of course I'm wobbly, it's Wobblesday today, isn't it?"

"No, it's Wednesday," said Ellen.

"Call it that if you like," said Mirror-Belle, waddling out of the Mirror Hall on her short legs, "but where *I* come from it's a Wobblesday, and everyone wobbles on Wobblesdays. It's a rule my father the King made. Even the *palace* goes wobbly on Wobblesdays. A bit like that one," she added, pointing to a bouncy castle on which some children were jumping about. The finger Mirror-Belle was pointing with looked like a wiggly knitting needle and Ellen laughed again. She found she was really glad to see Mirror-Belle after all. She hadn't exactly been looking forward to going on the ghost train by herself.

"Have you got any money?" Ellen asked. Mirror-Belle had three 50p and two 20p pieces.

"Exactly the same as me," said Ellen. "But all the writing is back to front on your coins."

"It's *yours* that are the wrong way round, silly," said Mirror-Belle.

They each gave 50p to the man in charge of the ghost train, who was chewing gum and staring at nothing. He didn't seem to notice Mirror-Belle's strange appearance or the backwards writing.

They got into a carriage of the ghost train behind a woman and a little boy.

"It'll be fun travelling on an ordinary train," said Mirror-Belle. "I've only ever been on a royal one before."

"This one isn't exactly *ordinary*—" Ellen warned, but was interrupted by an eerie voice:

"This is your Guaaaaaard speaking," the voice moaned. "Ride if you dare but prepare for a scare."

"What a silly guard!" said Mirror-Belle. "Why doesn't he tell us what stations we'll be going to and whether we can get tea and snacks on the train?"

The train set off. Almost immediately it plunged into a tunnel. As they turned a corner a luminous monster popped out at them. A little girl in front screamed.

"This is disgraceful, frightening inno-
cent children!" said Mirror-Belle. As she
spoke, a huge spider dangled down from
the ceiling and the girl screamed again.

"Don't they ever sweep their tunnels?"
said Mirror-Belle.

She reached up and grabbed the spider
with her long wiggly fingers.

"Go and build your web somewhere
else," she said, throwing it over her
shoulder. The people in the seats behind
screamed.

The train turned another corner, where
a ghost loomed out of the darkness and
went "Whooo!" at the little girl. She

clutched her mother.

"This is too bad," said Mirror-Belle. She leaned out of the carriage and went "Whooo!" back at the ghost, only much louder. The little girl turned round, saw Mirror-Belle and screamed again. Ellen wasn't surprised: with her gaping mouth and dangling chin Mirror-Belle probably looked like another ghost or monster to the little girl.

A few skeletons, vampires and coffins later the train stopped, and the little girl stopped screaming. "Can we have another go?" she said to her mother.

Mirror-Belle looked around her in disgust. "This is ridiculous," she said. "We haven't gone anywhere at all – we're back where we started. I'm going to complain to the stationmaster." She got out and headed towards the gum-chewing man, but Ellen managed to stop her.

"Why don't we have a go at the hoop-la?" she said. "Look, we could win one of those giant teddies."

Ellen had never won a prize at hoopla. She could never manage to throw her hoop over a peg so that it landed flat, and this time was no different. But for Mirror-Belle it was easy. She just reached out one of her amazingly long arms and put the hoop over the peg. Soon she had won three teddies and a goldfish in a bowl. A little crowd had gathered around them.

"Here, you take these," said Mirror-Belle, thrusting the teddies and goldfish at Ellen and moving on to the coconut shy. The crowd followed.

The man at the coconut shy looked

pleased to see so many people. Ellen missed with her three balls but Mirror-Belle's long arm reached almost to the stands holding the coconuts and she knocked them out with no trouble. The crowd grew bigger and some of the people started having goes. The coconut man didn't seem to mind Mirror-Belle winning so often, and even gave her a sack to put the teddies and coconuts in.

"I think you'd better stop before it gets too heavy to carry," said Ellen. "Do you like candyfloss?"

"Wobbably," said Mirror-Belle.

"Don't you mean, 'probably'?"

"No, I mean *wobbably*. That means that if the candyfloss is wobbly I'll like it. You seem to have forgotten that this is Wobblesday. On Wobblesdays we only eat wobbly food."

It took some time to reach the candy-floss stall, as Mirror-Belle could only take tiny steps with her short legs, while her long body wobbled about all over the place.

Mirror-Belle asked for two wobbly candyflosses. The candyfloss seller gave her a funny look but she wiggled the sticks about a lot as she spun the pink stuff round them, and Mirror-Belle decided that would do. Her mouth was so huge that she ate hers in one mouthful and asked for five more.

"I've got yards and yards of tummy to fill, you see," she said, after she'd eaten all five at once.

By now all their money was used up, and Ellen remembered she was supposed to be meeting Luke at the Mirror Hall. They went back there.

Outside the Mirror Hall there was a

sign saying, "Wobbly Mirror-Hall, 20p."

"*Really!*" said Mirror-Belle. "As if it's not bad enough everything being in backwards writing, they can't even spell my name."

She took a felt-tip pen out of her pocket, changed two of the letters and added one. The sign now said, "Wobbly Mirror-Belle, 20p".

"Now, Ellen," she said, "you collect the

WOBBLY MIRROR ~ Belle

money. Remember, it's twenty pence a wobble." She took up a position beside the notice, standing completely still, as if she was playing Musical Statues.

Ellen shuffled from foot to foot, not sure what to do. A few people gathered round.

"Twenty pence for what?" asked one.

"To see her wobble," said Ellen.

"She can't wobble, she's just a statue," said another.

"Isn't she that funny girl that was winning all the coconuts?" asked someone else.

In the end a man handed Ellen 20p, saying he wanted it back if he wasn't satisfied. As Ellen's palm closed round the coin, Mirror-Belle's body began to ripple, like a snake-charmer's snake rearing out of its basket and writhing about. She kept it up for half a minute and then stopped abruptly.

Immediately someone else gave Ellen 20p, and this time Mirror-Belle stretched out one of her long snaky arms. The crowd watched it wobble, curving and bending and eventually tying itself into a knot. Everyone clapped, except for one man who muttered, "It's all done with mirrors," in a knowing way.

The third time, Mirror-Belle wobbled her ears. They bounced up and down like yo-yos, nearly hitting the ground and then springing back up again. By this

time the crowd was quite big, and everybody seemed to be reaching into their pockets.

Then Ellen noticed Luke strolling towards them from a ride called Jaws of Terror, his gelled hair glinting in the sunshine.

"Here comes my brother!" she said to Mirror-Belle.

With one last bounce of her ears Mirror-Belle turned and waddled, surprisingly quickly, into the Mirror Hall.

"Hey, you haven't paid!" the attendant called out.

"I'll pay for her," said Ellen. She gave the attendant two of the three 20ps they had earned, and followed Mirror-Belle, but she was overtaken by several of the crowd, eager for more wobbly stunts. Ellen looked around for Mirror-Belle but couldn't find her. Instead, she bumped into Luke.

"There you are!" he said. "You don't know what you've missed! That Space-Lurcher — it's amazing the way it stops and changes direction just when you're upside down at the top. You really feel you're going to fall out." Then he noticed the goldfish bowl and the sack. He looked inside the sack and saw the teddies and coconuts.

"Did you win all those?" he asked. Ellen could tell he was trying not to sound too impressed. She nearly said, "No, Mirror-Belle did," but she knew Luke wouldn't believe her. She guessed, too, that Mirror-Belle would by now have made her getaway into one of the wobbly mirrors. So instead she answered, "Yes — and I've still got twenty pence left!"

Chapter Six

LOVE-POTION CRISPS

It was the first day of term and Ellen was starting at her new school. Mum took her to the head teacher's office, and the head teacher took her to her classroom.

"This is Ellen, who is going to be joining your class," she announced. All the other children stared at Ellen. She clutched her lunch box tightly and tried to smile.

"Hello, Ellen," said the teacher brightly. "Perhaps you'd like to hang your blazer up in the cloakroom next door? You'll find a peg in there with your name on it."

Ellen found her peg and hung up her blazer. Underneath it she wore a tunic and blouse, and a tie with diagonal green and yellow stripes. Her old school didn't have a uniform, so she had never worn a tie before. She checked in the cloakroom mirror to make sure it was straight.

Yes, the tie looked fine but, oh dear, Ellen didn't feel like going back into the classroom and being stared at again.

She was just turning away from the mirror when a voice said, "You *do* look

worried. Never fear, I'll be there."

Ellen turned back in time to see Mirror-Belle stepping cheerfully out of the mirror. She carried a lunch box just like Ellen's and was wearing the same uniform, except that the stripes in her tie sloped in the opposite direction.

"Mirror-Belle! *You* can't come to school with me!" said Ellen.

"What do you mean, I can't? I just have, haven't I?" said Mirror-Belle. She skipped past Ellen out of the cloakroom and opened the classroom door.

"Hello again, Ellen," said the teacher, and then looked surprised as she saw the real Ellen behind Mirror-Belle.

"I didn't know you had a twin," she said.

"Well, never mind," said Mirror-Belle. "You can't know everything. I don't suppose you know how many fairy godmothers I've got either."

"Now, Ellen, don't be cheeky," said the teacher.

"That's something else you don't know," said Mirror-Belle. "I'm not Ellen, I'm Mirror-Belle."

"Very well, Mirror-Belle, now come and sit down at this table. You and Ellen can be in Orange group."

"I'd rather be in Gold group or Silver group," said Mirror-Belle.

"We don't have either of those, I'm afraid," said the teacher firmly, "but I'm sure you'll get on fine in Orange group if you behave yourself."

She gave out some exercise books and asked the children to write about what they had done in the holidays. Ellen wrote about moving house.

The teacher wandered round the class-room. She came over to Orange group's table and looked over Mirror-Belle's shoulder.

"Yours is a bit difficult to read, Mirror-Belle," she said. "Your letters seem to be the wrong way round. It is easy to get muddled up, I know, especially between 'b's and 'd's."

"Oh, poor you," said Mirror-Belle. "Do you really get as muddled up as all that? Don't worry – I'm sure you'll learn. Perhaps you'd better use a mirror to read my writing."

"That's quite a good idea," said the teacher, and took a mirror out of her handbag. "Yes, I can read it fine now. Mirror-Belle's written a very interesting story," she told the class. "Do you mind if I read it out, Mirror-Belle?"

"Not at all," said Mirror-Belle. "I expect you could do with a bit of reading practice."

The teacher read out Mirror-Belle's story. It went like this:

"I didn't do very much in the holidays because I got turned into a golden statue. You see, my father the King was nice to an old man and so he was given the power to turn everything he touched to gold. By mistake he touched me. In the end I got turned back by being washed in a magic river."

The children all laughed at this story, and the teacher said, "That was good, Mirror-Belle, although I seem to have heard that story before somewhere. What I asked you to write about was what you *really* did in the holidays."

"But I told you, I didn't *do* anything," said Mirror-Belle. "You *can't* when you're a golden statue – you can't move, or eat or brush your hair or anything. I had this awful tickle on my leg and I couldn't even scratch it."

At this point the bell for morning play rang. A friendly girl called Katy took Ellen and Mirror-Belle into the playground where they joined in a game of tig. But two big boys kept bumping into Ellen. They pretended it was by accident but Ellen could tell it was on purpose.

"That's Bruce Baxter and Stephen Hodge," said Katy. "They're *always* like that." Mirror-Belle said nothing but looked very thoughtful.

After playtime the teacher gave out some maths books and asked the children to turn to a page which had a picture of a fruit shop.

"Now," she said, "if one apple costs ten pence and Susan gives the fruit-seller fifty pence, how much change will she get?"

"Hold on a second," said Mirror-Belle. "Look at those apples. Would you say they're half red and half green?"

"What about it, Mirror-Belle?"

"I think Susan ought to watch out," said Mirror-Belle. "How does she know the apple-selling lady hasn't poisoned the apples? She's probably a wicked queen in disguise, trying to get rid of anyone more beautiful than her."

"*Mirror-Belle!*" said the teacher angrily. "I'm not asking you to tell fairy stories. I asked how much *change* Susan would get from her fifty pence. How much do you think?"

"None," said Mirror-Belle. "If that queen's as wicked as I think she is, she'll run off with the fifty pence."

By the time the bell rang for lunch the teacher was looking quite exhausted.

In the dinner hall Ellen and Mirror-Belle sat with Katy and the other children who had brought packed lunches. Unfortunately, these included Bruce Baxter and Stephen Hodge. When the dinner lady wasn't looking Bruce grabbed Ellen's bag of crisps. Then Stephen took Katy's chocolate bar and Bruce snatched another child's yogurt.

They put all the things in a bag along with some other goodies they had stolen.

"They always do that," said Katy. "Then they eat them in the playground."

"But why don't you tell the dinner lady?" asked Ellen.

"If you do that they lie in wait on the way home from school and pounce on you."

Once again Mirror-Belle was being unusually quiet and thoughtful. She had managed to avoid having her lunch stolen, and she took an unopened packet of crisps out into the playground. They looked just like Ellen's crisps except for the writing being back to front.

Katy and her friends had a long skipping rope and they asked Ellen and Mirror-Belle to play with them. But Bruce Baxter and Stephen Hodge kept barging into the game and treading on the rope. Stephen was swinging the bag of stolen food. Just as they were interrupting the game for the fourth time, Mirror-Belle said loudly, "I see I've got love-potion-flavoured crisps today."

"What are they?" said Ellen.

"They make you fall in love with the first person you see."

She popped one into her mouth, fixing her eyes on Bruce Baxter.

"Oh, my hero!" she suddenly exclaimed. Then she ran up to him and hugged him. Bruce went red. All the girls laughed at him and so did Stephen.

"Let me shower you with kisses!" said Mirror-Belle, aiming a kiss at Bruce's nose. He turned away and the kiss landed on his ear.

"You were so wonderful when you were spoiling the skipping game," she said. "*Please* do it again and I'll give you *ten* kisses!"

"Leave me alone," said Bruce.

"Never!" cried Mirror-Belle. She bit into another crisp, at the same time staring at Stephen Hodge. "Oh, my darling!" she said. "My own true love!" She threw her arms around Stephen and this time it was his turn to go red.

"You're so *clever* to have taken all that food. You *won't* give it back, will you?"

"Come on, let's go!" said Stephen to Bruce, looking very embarrassed.

"Where you go I follow!" said Mirror-Belle. "The only way to break the spell is to give me a bag of food, but I'm sure you won't want to do that, will you?"

The boys dumped the bag at Mirror-Belle's feet and ran off.

After Mirror-Belle had given the food

back to its owners the skipping game started up again, this time undisturbed.

"Are those *really* magic crisps?" asked Katy.

"Try one and see!" said Mirror-Belle.

Katy ate a crisp and so did Ellen, but neither of them fell in love with anyone.

"Perhaps it only works on princesses," said Mirror-Belle.

Back in the classroom the teacher got the paints out and told the children to roll up their sleeves and put aprons on.

"We're going to do a project on pets this term," she said. "I'd like you all to paint a picture of a pet. It can either be your own pet or one belonging to a friend."

Ellen started on a picture of her goldfish. The teacher came over to their table.

"That's good, Ellen," she said. "I like those wiggly water weeds." She looked at Mirror-Belle's paper. "I see you're painting two animals, Mirror-Belle. What are they? A dog and a cat?"

"No," said Mirror-Belle, "a lion and a unicorn."

"What an imagination you've got!"

said the teacher.

"It's not me who's got the imagination, it's them!" said Mirror-Belle. "For some reason they both seem to imagine they should be sitting on the throne instead of my father. They're always fighting for the crown. It's a wonder they haven't torn each other to pieces by now."

But the teacher had stopped listening and was looking instead at Mirror-Belle's

hands and arms. They were covered in yellow splodges.

"You've got an awful lot of paint on yourself, Mirror-Belle," she said.

"Oh dear me," said Mirror-Belle. "That's not paint – I think I'm turning into gold again! I thought I was feeling a bit peculiar. I'll have to have a dip in that magic river before I get solid."

"I'm sure you'll find the tap water in the cloakroom will do the job, Mirror-Belle," the teacher said sternly. "And if you're still feeling peculiar after that you can go to the medical room."

"How could I get there if I've turned to gold?" asked Mirror-Belle, as she left the classroom.

Ten minutes later, when she still hadn't come back, the teacher sent Ellen into the cloakroom. Ellen wasn't surprised at what she found. Mirror-Belle had gone, and the cloakroom mirror was covered in smears of yellow paint. On the floor Ellen found a scrap of paper with some backwards writing on it. She held it up to the mirror and read:

Dear Ellen, Sorry I had to go. Love Mirror-Belle. P.S. Give Bruce Baxter and Stephen Hodge a kiss each from me.

Mirror-Belle never came back to school. The head teacher wrote a letter to Ellen's mum saying, *You only enrolled one child at our school, and we feel that your other child might fit in better somewhere else.* Ellen's mum thought this was rather strange.

"I wasn't thinking of sending Luke to Ellen's school – he's too old, in any case," she said.

Ellen made some friends at school and soon stopped feeling shy. But she never gave Bruce or Stephen their kiss from Mirror-Belle because they didn't come anywhere near her.

Bruce and Stephen weren't taking any chances. The new girl looked normal. As far as they could tell her crisps were normal. She said she was called Ellen. But maybe – just maybe – she was really Mirror-Belle.

Julia Donaldson

A wicked wolf on the prowl

Two clever crooks in search of loot

A beautiful girl imprisoned in the underworld

From traditional to modern, from fantasy
to fun, there's a part for everyone in this
brilliant collection of eleven short plays
written by bestselling author Julia Donaldson.

Perfect for primary school or family use,
and suitable for a wide variety of ages and abilities,
Play Time provides everything the budding actor needs to
raise the curtain on the wonderful world of theatre!